Out-of-this-world Events

KELL

AND THE

GIANTS

THE ALIENS, INC. SERIES
BOOK 3

KELL AND THE GIANTS

By Darcy Pattison

pictures by
Rich Davis

MIMS HOUSE / LITTLE ROCK, AR

Mims House
1309 S. Broadway
Little Rock, AR 72202

www.mimshouse.com.com

Publisher's Note: This is a work of fiction. Names, characters, places, and incidents are a product of the author's imagination. Locales and public names are sometimes used for atmospheric purposes. Any resemblance to actual people, living or dead, or to businesses, companies, events, institutions, or locales is completely coincidental.

Book design © 2013 by BookDesignTemplates.com

Kell, the Alien/ Darcy Pattison — First Edition
Library of Congress Control Number: 2014906313
Paperback ISBN 978-1-62944-026-2
Library Paperback ISBN 978-149748-025-4
Hardcover ISBN 978-1-62944-025-5
Ebook ISBN 978-1-62944-027-9
Lexile 540L
Printed in the United States of America

Thanks to Todd Hutcheson for his help with superheroes. You are a Hulk!

CHAPTER

I bent over the giant state of Texas.

"Texas is so big," said Mrs. Crux the art teacher, "that I need three students to work together to paint it: Bree, Roman and Kell."

Our art class was painting a map of the United States on the basketball court. Alaska needed three people to paint it, too. Most

kids were painting just one state. Some students had two small states to color. One student was painting five small states.

Roman East dabbed red paint on the south Texas beaches and said, "We need to plan my birthday party. I want a Giant party."

I asked, "How big a party do you want?"

"No," Roman said. "Not a big party. A party about giants. You know, really tall people."

Roman was the tallest kid in third grade. I could understand why he was interested in giants.

I swiped red paint onto the Panhandle of north Texas.

Meanwhile, Bree Hendricks, my best friend, was painting red on the east side of Texas. She said, "No one knows anything about giants. Name one giant."

Roman said, "There was Cyclops, the one-eyed giant. Paul Bunyan was an American giant who lived in the forests and cut down giant trees. In the Bible, a boy named David killed a nine-foot giant named Goliath."

Bree giggled and said, "I just remembered a giant. There's the Jolly Green Giant who wears green underwear."

I frowned. I had only read about Atlas, the giant who is supposed to hold the world on his shoulders. Before my family crash-landed, we got a good look at Earth from space. There isn't really a giant holding up the Earth. That Atlas story, it's just a folktale.

The art class was working outside in the wide-open spaces. And sure enough, a flying bug found me. It zoomed around my ears and then flew high enough to be out of reach. Quick, I dropped to my knees and hissed at Bree, "What kind of bug?"

Her head circled, following the bug above my head. "It's a honeybee. It's OK. Don't smash it."

Slowly, I peeked upward, and the bee dropped a couple inches closer. Terrified, I held very, very, very still. On Earth, there are more bugs than any other kind of animal. I don't like Earth bugs. You never knew when a bug might bite or sting you. This one had a black head, a golden body, and a stinger.

I waved at the honeybee to go away. It just circled my head again. I shivered and ducked.

Just then, Mrs. Lynx, the principal, came out of the school building and trotted over to us. She wore her toe shoes, so she ran very quietly. Running beside her was a dog about as tall as her knees. The dog had a brown head, ears, and neck, but the back part of him was spotted. They stopped at the edge of the map, and Mrs. Lynx said, "Sit."

The dog sat.

Meanwhile, the honeybee was gone, flying away when I wasn't looking. That didn't fool me. I knew it would be back.

"Be careful," Mrs. Crux said. "The paint is still wet."

Mrs. Lynx frowned. "Then how are they getting out of Texas?"

Bree and I backed into each other and then Roman bumped into us. We had painted ourselves into the very center of Texas. There was no way out!

Bree said, "It's OK. We can jump. Kell and I are good at hopscotch."

I groaned. I am an alien from the planet Bix. I can do telekinesis, which means I can move things with my mind. Bree wanted me to give her a boost when she jumped. But Mrs. Lynx is President of the S.A.C., the Society of Alien Chasers. If I helped Bree too much, Mrs. Lynx would suspect that I was an alien.

Still, we were trapped in Texas.

Mrs. Crux said, "Are you sure, mate, that you can jump far enough?" She is from Australia and says "mate" all the time.

Bree nodded and said, "I will jump on three."

"1, 2, 3!" She leapt high—with a little help from a Bix alien—and landed on the tennis court away from the paint.

"You next," I told Roman.

"I can't jump that far," Roman said. He has long legs and I thought he might even be able to take a giant step to get out of Texas. But he wouldn't try. Instead, he bent and leapt. He's so big and clumsy that he really needed a boost! He landed just outside Texas and fell into a heap.

Roman cried out, "What was that?" He twisted around to stare at me.

Oh, no! He must have felt me giving him a shove.

Quickly, Bree said, "You're a great jumper!"

He stood up and brushed off his shirt. Looking at the distance he had jumped, he stood a bit taller. "I'm a better jumper than I thought."

Now, I had to jump. I bent and leapt.

But right in mid-air—BZZZ! Three honeybees zipped around me. I slapped at them and forgot to do telekinesis. I fell onto the south beaches of Texas.

"Do you want me to give you jumping lessons?" Roman said. Smiling at his own joke, he held out a hand, and I took it.

Roman pulled me up halfway, but we got stuck. He pulled and I pulled, but I didn't go any farther. I was just hanging over Texas.

I pulled so hard that my arms were tired and shaky. Roman's arms were shaking, too.

And then, Roman dropped me!

"No!" I cried. Plop! I was back in the wet paint.

Roman swung his arms around to make them feel better. But the rest of the class just pointed and laughed. I dropped my face to my knees and groaned.

Roman bent down and this time grabbed my right hand with both of his hands. He jerked hard and I tumbled onto the basketball court. I pushed myself up and tried to stand.

"Look at his pants!"

"His butt is red!"

Across the giant map of the United States, kids laughed. I was so upset. To hide the red paint, I sat down on a blue bench.

Freddy Rubin yelled at me, "NO!"

What? Quick, I stood up and looked around.

Oh, no. The bench was splotched with red paint from where I sat. It was times like this that I longed for my home planet of Bix. On Bix, red is the color of the sky. That red splotch on the blue bench left an ache, a longing to see the skies of Bix.

Mrs. Crux smiled at me, "Again, mate?"

Sadly, I nodded. It was my 14th Accidental Art.

Mrs. Crux handed me a small paintbrush. "Why don't you just sign your name? I'll take a picture of it for the Accidental Art bulletin

board. You can go to the office and call your mom to bring you new pants."

With a sigh, I took the brush and took some black paint offered by Aja. I painted my name on the bench beside my butt-print: Kell Smith. I may be an alien, but I'm not dumb. I made sure the name was smeared so badly that no one could read it.

Meanwhile, Mrs. Crux bent to pet Mrs. Lynx's dog. "When did you get her?"

Mrs. Lynx's eyes lit up. "My brother, Ernest, brought her yesterday. She's a German shorthaired pointer. He trained Gloria, and she's the best alien pointer dog in the world."

"What does a pointer do?"

"When she smells an alien," Mrs. Lynx said, "she points and holds that point until I find the right person."

Oh, no! I thought. It was never safe with Mrs. Lynx around. She and the S.A.C. kept trying to catch an alien. Someday, she would catch my family and me.

Roman walked over to look at the dog. "May I pet her?"

"Yes," Mrs. Lynx said.

Roman squatted down and starting scratching the dog behind her ears.

Mrs. Lynx said, "Roman, I hear you're going to have a Giant birthday party. Aliens, Inc. does a great job with parties."

"Yes, ma'am," Roman said. "I hope we have stilts And maybe Big Foot can come."

I needed a Look-Up Later list for a Giant party:

LOOK UP LATER LIST FOR GIANTS

1. What are stilts?
2. Who are Cyclops, Paul Bunyan, Goliath, and Big Foot?

Just then the bell rang, and it was time to go inside. I would go by the office and call Mom to bring me a change of clothes. Bree and I walked way around the other side of the basketball court to stay far away from the alien pointer dog named Gloria. But Gloria was watching me. She didn't fool me.

She smelled me and sooner or later, she would point me out.

"Hey, I have a riddle for you," Bree said.

"OK."

"What is the best tasting throw-up?"

"Yuk," I said. "No throw up tastes good."

"Wrong," Bree said. "Honeybees eat nectar and then throw up honey."

That Bree. Earth girls are full of odd facts.

CHAPTER 2

At home, Bree and I made peanut butter sandwiches and ate them on the back deck. Just as we finished, we heard Dad's truck pull in. Dad staggered into the back yard, his arms wrapped around a stack of three white boxes. Awkwardly, he set them beside the greenhouse.

Mom followed him and set down a plastic bag. She pulled out some white clothes. "Look what we got!"

Bree's eyes got wide. "Is that bee keeper clothes?"

Mom shook out a white hat and slipped it on. A fine net fell down around her neck and chest. "Yes," she said. "With these clothes on, the bees can't sting me."

Dad stood and gestured to the boxes. "Our first bee hive."

I stared at my parents like they were aliens. "Why on Earth would you want a bee hive?"

"It's another way to make money," Mom said. "I already grow flowers, and bees make honey from flowers. We can sell the honey, and we will have money to buy food."

Our space ship crashed on Earth a year ago, and we were still figuring out how to make a living. We sold our space ship to buy our house, and the Aliens, Inc. party business was good. Still, Mom worried about food, electricity, and other bills.

"Mom," I said, "honeybees are bugs."

"Bees are OK if you handle them right," Mom said.

Mom was so excited, I couldn't say anything else.

Then I remembered: "Mrs. Lynx has a new dog. It's supposed to be able to smell an alien."

Dad frowned. "Did you get close to the dog?"

"It was across the basketball court from us," Bree said. "We stayed far away."

"But it will be hard to stay away from it all the time," I said.

Dad's face looked grim.

Just then, the doorbell rang. Because Mom is outside in her greenhouse a lot, Dad had put a ringer out here, too.

Bree and I ran around the house and found Roman and his Dad there. If Roman was the tallest kid in our class, his Dad was the tallest Earthling I had ever seen. He was six foot nine inches tall, a basketball star in college.

"Come out back," I said.

We sat on the back deck and talked about the Giant party.

Mr. East stretched out his long legs and I stared at his giant shoes.

He said, "I've never used a party planner before."

"We just need to know what you want," Mom said.

She was getting better at talking to people about parties.

"Because we just moved to town, we want to invite Roman's whole class," Mr. East said. "He'll make friends that way."

Dad asked, "Mr. East, what do you do?"

"I'm a doctor."

"Oh," I said. "You're Dr. East, not Mr. East."

He nodded.

Aliens don't like Earthling doctors. If Dr. East x-rayed my body, he wouldn't find a stomach or a heart. He'd find a *bligfa* and other alien body parts.

"What kind of doctor?" Bree asked.

There are different kinds of doctors? I didn't know that. I guess there would be doctors for Earthling hearts and doctors for Earthling brains and doctors for Earthling feet.

"I work at the university and do research," Dr. East said.

On Bix, Dad is an astro-physicist and does research, too.

He asked, "What projects are you working on?"

"Right now, I'm working on a comparison of humans to gorillas."

"Comparative biology?" Mom said. "You want to know how humans and gorillas are the same and how they are different."

"Yes," said Dr. East.

"OK," Dad said. "But how are you comparing them?"

"I have studied the human body," he said, "but I've also taken veterinary classes. I am interested in giant animals. Elephants, giraffes, pythons. Why do some animals grow so big?"

Roman laughed and said, "He's worried about me. Mom is six foot four, and he thinks I might be close to seven feet tall when I'm all grown."

Dr. East laughed, "I'm not worried about you, Roman. It's just that when you're a giant, you get interested in giant things."

Bree nodded. "If you were an alien, you might be interested in alien things."

"Exactly," Dr. East said.

I glared at Bree for talking about aliens, but she turned to Roman.

"For your party, do you want basketball games?" she said.

"Yes! But I also want things like giant jawbreakers."

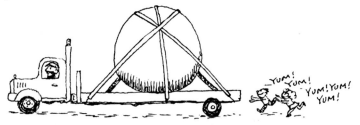

Mom's forehead wrinkled. "You want to break the jaws of your friends?"

Dr. East laughed. "That's a good joke."

Mom laughed, too, but she didn't understand the joke. I would have to explain later.

Dr. East said, "You could do giant balloons or top hats to make kids seem even taller. And I have basketball friends who can dress up like giants."

I added to my Giant Look Up Later list:

3. What is a jawbreaker?

4. Where do you get giant balloons or top hats?

After a while, Dr. East stood and said, "My wife, Mikki, will be waiting supper for us. We need to go."

Dad and Mom walked them out to their car while I walked Bree to her house.

Bree asked, "What do you think of your mom's beehives?

I shuddered. But I didn't want Bree to know I was scared. So I asked a dumb question: "Here's a comparative biology question. Do bees sleep like Earthlings and aliens?"

Bree said, "Yes, bees sleep. They get very still and don't move for a long time and their brains take a rest."

"Is that the truth, the whole truth and nothing but the truth?" I asked.

"Yes. I did a research report on honeybees last year." Bree hit my shoulder and ran up the front steps into her house.

Wait. Why did she hit me? I will never understand Earthling girls.

CHAPTER 3

O n Mr. Martinez's desk stood something tall that was covered with a red cloth. On the far wall of the Social Studies room, a giant map hung from the ceiling. Mr. Martinez pointed a red laser at the map's key.

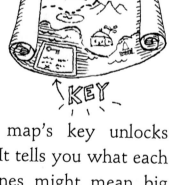

Key is an odd Earthling word. Keys are metal things that unlock doors. But a map's key unlocks information on a map. It tells you what each symbol means. Red lines might mean big roads, and blue lines might mean bigger roads. To understand a map, you have to look at its key.

Mr. Martinez turned, and the red laser flashed over our heads and jerked around. He turned it off and said, "In two weeks, we will have a Geography Day. Your job is to draw a map. You can draw a map of your neighborhood or your city. Or maybe a map of the school. The winner will receive this." He pulled the red cloth off the tall thing on his desk.

It was a globe, which is a ball that looks like the planet Earth. But this ball was black with silver dots for stars. Some stars were

connected with lines to show the constellations.

"See the night stars as you've never seen them before."

Mr. Martinez flipped a switch on the globe's cord, and it lit up inside. The stars twinkled, small pinpricks of light. Wow! It was great.

Mr. Martinez said, "The student with the best map on Geography Day will win this star globe."

I had to win that prize! I have studied stars all my life. I know the names of all the major stars. Well, the Bix names. Earthlings call their star, Sol. But on Bix we called Earth's star Ixfar, which means "small."

At lunch, everyone argued about the star globe.

"I'll win it," Freddy said. "Someday, I'll live on the moon, and I need to know about space and stars to get there."

"We'll see about that," Bree said. "The star globe is mine. I want to meet an alien someday, and I need something to talk about."

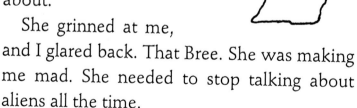

She grinned at me, and I glared back. That Bree. She was making me mad. She needed to stop talking about aliens all the time.

Mary Lee said, "I need a night light."

"Stars. Night light," Bree laughed. "I get it."

Aja and Edgar were making 5-pointed stars out of French fries.

"You know," Bree said, "stars don't really have points."Edgar nodded. "Duh. They are balls of fire."

Aja scooped up one French fry star—all five points—and stuffed it into his mouth. "Ow!" he joked. "It's burning hot!"

Aja, Edgar, Freddy, Roman and I all laughed. Bree and Mary Lee rolled their eyes.

Edgar said, "I have a star globe already. And a telescope. I don't need that one."

"Hey, can we come and look through your telescope sometime?" Bree said. "I want to see alien worlds up close."

Aliens! There she was talking about aliens again. Why did she do that?

Edgar nodded. "Whenever you want."

"I need to win that star globe," Roman said. "I've never won anything before, and it's my turn."

Roman's eyes were dark and starless. They looked sad. It made me sad, too.

Aja swallowed the fries and took a drink. He said, "I need that star globe as a present for my Mom. In three weeks, it's her 40th birthday, and I want her to feel like a star on her special day."

Quietly Bree started singing to herself.

"What song is that?" Mary Lee asked.

"Twinkle, Twinkle," Bree said.

"Oh! I like that one." The girls picked up their food trays walked away to put them up. But I heard them singing together—a duet!

Twinkle, twinkle, little star
How I wonder what you are.
Up above the world so high
Like a diamond in the sky.

I followed them with my food tray, just so I could listen to Bree sing. How did she always know so many words for songs? She must memorize things easily. Now this is the truth, the whole truth and nothing but the truth: when Bree sings, the Earth sun comes out and shines in my heart. It takes away all sadness.

I thought about that star globe. My Earthling friends all had good Earthling reasons to want the star globe. I wanted it because I'm not an Earthling. I belong to the stars.

Would I ever see Bix again? Or would I always live on Earth? I had good Earthling friends. But did I have a real home here on Earth or not? I didn't know.

That night, I decided that drawing a map is hard. First you have to know landmarks, or big places. Then you have to know how far it is from one landmark to another. How are the landmarks connected? With a bicycle path or a street or a river?

I took my drawing paper and climbed up into the biggest tree house where Dad was sitting.

"Are you sleeping up here tonight?" I asked.

"Not tonight," he said. "I'm just star gazing." On Bix, we live in tree houses, so Dad had built five tree houses in our back yard. When he gets homesick, he sleeps in one of them.

"I need help drawing a map." I explained about Geography Day and the star globe.

"When we did the Friends of Police parade, you drew the parade map." In the fading light, his eyes were a warm grey. "You don't need help. You just need to do it."

Dad was right. But this time, I wanted everything to be perfect because I needed to win that star globe. But I thought about my friends and how much they wanted to win the star globe. Did I want to beat them? And if I won, would I brag to them about winning?

I lay on my back in Dad's tree house and watched the stars. There were bright constellations that the Earthlings called the Big Dipper, the Small Dipper and my favorite, Orion, the giant.

Did I need a star globe to be from the stars?

No. I was from the stars whether or not I won Geography Day.

Maybe I should make maps for each of my friends. No way! That would be too many maps! Each map would need to be different because each friend wanted the star globe for a different reason. How would I have time to do that and help plan a Giant Party at the same time? I didn't know, but I wanted to try.

Lights were shining in Bree's house next door. Would she think it was odd if I gave everyone a map? Did Earthlings ever do something nice for their friends—just because they were friends?

CHAPTER 4

All that week, Mrs. Lynx and Gloria patrolled the hallways looking for aliens. Our school has three main hallways with the school office in the middle. The Kindergarten hallway is short and just has kindergarten classrooms, plus the computer lab, music room and art room. The Lower Grades Hallway has 1st, 2nd, and 3rd grade classrooms. The Upper Grades Hallway has 4th, 5th and 6th grade classrooms. Starting at the office, Mrs. Lynx and Gloria walked up and down the three hallways.

After each trip down a hallway, Mrs. Lynx stopped to study the U.S. map that hung outside the Principal's Office. Green alien stickers marked all the places where someone had seen an alien. Our city didn't have a sticker.

ALIENS ARE HERE!!

Gloria always walked with held her head high. Her eyes were bright, and her tail often wagged. I kept wondering, did aliens really smell different from humans? Because what scared me was Gloria's black, shiny nose.

After I told Mom about Gloria, she decided I needed to smell better. On Monday, I wore my Dad's cologne. On Tuesday, I smelled like the lemon juice that Mom used to wash my hair. And on Wednesday, my skin started peeling. It does that once a month at least, and I smell different when I am about to shed my skin.

"P-yew! What is that smell?" Freddy asked at lunch on Thursday.

Bree jerked her thumb at me. "He keeps trying different smells."

"This one is bad!" Aja said. "What is it?"

"It's a bug  repellent," I said. "Mom has beehives now, and I am keeping the honeybees away."

"Everyone will stay away from that smell. It is a people repellent, too," Edgar said.

I just wanted a dog repellent to keep Gloria away. Meanwhile, my skin was itching and itching. It would be a day or two before it all peeled away.

I had to do something about Gloria because I didn't want to wear new smells every day. Then I thought about how much Aja loved French fries. After school, Bree and I stopped at a pet store and bought doggie treats and zip-lock bags. I filled up bags with doggie treats and gave them to my friends. Now, whenever we could, we snuck treats to Gloria.

Once Mrs. Lynx was talking to another teacher. Edgar rolled his wheelchair close and stopped next to the dog. He let his hand hang out over the wheel, and Gloria nudged his hand for the treat.

Another time we were lined up and waiting outside the computer lab. Mrs. Lynx and Gloria came down the hall, and Aja dropped his pencil right in front of them. Mrs. Lynx stopped to pick it up and hand it to Aja. Behind her back, Bree fed Gloria a treat.

Now, when she saw third graders coming, Gloria's tail wagged.

With the Gloria problem under control, it was time to work on the Giant party. On

Thursday after school, Mom drove Bree and me to the party store for ideas on the Giant party. We just had one week and one day before the Roman's party.

Mom, Bree and I walked in, and the party store was still dark and cluttered. Clothes racks held shiny costumes while masks covered every wall.  A man was behind a counter with his back to us.

Mom said, "Excuse me, sir."

The man turned and—a freak! The man only had one eye. It was a giant eye in the middle of his forehead.

I yelped and rushed for the door.

Behind me, Bree laughed. "You can't fool me again," she said.

Surprised, I turned back, and the man pulled up a one-eyed mask. It was Mr. Jasper. He said, "Smart girl."

Bree is a smart girl, but I am a dumb alien because that mask scared me.

Mom said, "Mr. Jasper, we need ideas for a game for a Giant party."

He said, "I have just the thing."

Mr. Jasper led us to the back of the store and stopped in front of a tall post. At the top was a metal circle, and at the bottom was a red circle. "This is the giant striker game," Mr. Jasper said. He handed me a long-handled hammer, waved at the red circle, and said, "Hit it."

I hefted the hammer and brought it down hard. CRASH!

On the post, a red arrow soared upward.

"Not hard enough," Mr. Jasper said. "You didn't ring the bell at the top. Only the strongest people can make the bell ring."

Mom said, "Let me try." She pushed up her shirtsleeves and picked up the hammer. "Stand back," she told Bree and me. Was this my Mom? Her arms had muscles!

Mom swung the hammer down hard. BANG! The red arrow shot upward. But not as high as mine.

Really? Mom couldn't ring the bell? This was odd.

The store man whistled. "Good try."

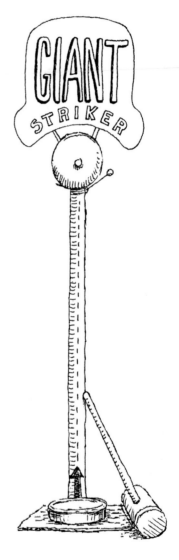

Mom frowned and pulled down her shirtsleeves. "That was harder than I thought."

Bree said, "May I try?"

Mr. Jasper handed the hammer to her and stepped back out of her way.

It was a giant hammer, and Bree is small. She struggled to get the hammer to her shoulder. Then, she shoved it off her shoulder and let it fall onto the red circle. "Bang!"

The red arrow shot up. And up and up and—DING! The bell at the top rang!

Odd, odd, odd, I thought.

Mom glared at the man. "How did you do that?"

"Do what?" The man was grinning.

"You are making it easier or harder to make the bell ring," Mom accused.

"Of course," he said. "I wanted you to understand how the tall striker works." He showed how to adjust the striker by stepping on a lever at the bottom of the game. It was easy to work without people seeing you do it.

"You cheated," Mom said.

Now Mr. Jasper frowned. "Oh no, Ma'am. If adults rent the game, they want it hard to ring the bell. When you rent the game for a kid's birthday party, you want it easy to ring the bell."

Bree said, "Oh." She bounced on her toes and told Mom, "We don't have to tell everyone that we can make it hard or easy."

"What do you mean?" Mom asked.

Bounce, bounce. Bree said, "Well, maybe my Dad doesn't have to know." Bounce, bounce.

I understood what Bree was thinking. The game would be easy for the kids. But we could trick our fathers and make it really hard for them to ring the bell. They would try harder and harder.

Mom grinned and said, "Kids, this is our secret."

And we grinned back.

That Bree. Earthling girls sure know how to plan a joke on Dads.

CHAPTER

I had decided to make five maps. One to turn in and one for each of my Earthling friends.

Freddy wants to live on the Earthling moon. I don't know why anyone would want to live on that cold rock, but if that's what he wanted I would help him. I drew him a map of the craters of the moon.

Bree wants to talk to aliens—like me. For that, she needs to know more about my home planet. On the left leg of the giant constellation of Orion is a bright star called Rigel. In fact, Rigel is three stars, Rigel A, Rigel B, and Rigel C. But from Earth, it looks like one bright star. That is my star system. Earthling scientists have only found about a thousand planets outside of their own solar system. So, they don't know about my planet yet. Bix is a planet that orbits around Rigel C. Mr. Martinez might think this was an imaginary solar system map, but he would be wrong. I am from Bix. It is there.

Aja and his mom were a big problem.

Mom was walking through the kitchen with her bee clothes on.

I asked her, "What do you get someone's Mom for her 40th birthday?"

She mumbled, "Something pretty."

She pulled on the white bee gloves and went out to look at her honeybees.

I found black paper and drew on

it with gold ink. I drew a beautiful map of our city and marked Aja's house on it.

Mary Lee was easy. I drew the Big Dipper and Little Dipper constellations. But I used glow-in-the-dark paint. If she hung the map on her bedroom ceiling, it would be a night-light.

Edgar didn't need a special star map because he already had a star globe and a telescope.

Roman was the hardest because he had never won anything before, and he really wanted to win. But that meant he had to have the best map of all. So, I had to help him draw his map.

I called Roman on the phone. "Will you help me with my map?"

"OK," Roman said.

That night at his house, I met his mom, and she is a giant, too. She popped corn for a snack while we worked. We spread out a huge paper on the floor, and Roman got out his markers.

"I will help you with your map first," I said. "Then we can do my map."

His map was like the U.S. map on the tennis courts. But Roman was sloppy. He drew crooked lines.

I said, "You draw the lines in pencil. I will draw on top of your lines with a big marker." That way, I could make the lines look better.

After an hour of work, we stopped, and Dr. East came in to take a look at the map. He folded his tall legs and sat on the floor and let us tell about the map.

"It only needs color now," Roman said.

Dr. East pulled him into a hug. "You've done a great job. Kell, thank you for helping."

Dr. East was pretty nice for a Dad, I thought.

The next afternoon at school, we were coming back from Music Class when we saw Mrs. Lynx and Gloria ahead of us. Mrs. Lynx knocked on a 2nd grade classroom door. She looked down at Gloria and said, "Let's find that alien."

The door opened, and she went inside. As we passed, I saw Gloria walking up and down the aisles between desks. She was sniffing at each student.

Oh no! I thought. Our classroom would be next.

"What can I do?" I asked Bree.

"Leave the room," she said.

"But Mrs. Lynx will catch me in the hallway."

"Then you have to time it right," Bree said.

She pulled me to the back of the homeroom. We pretended to be reading a book. Roman came to the back of the room, too.

"What's happening on my party?" he asked.

"It will be in my back yard," I said.

Roman frowned. "What if it rains?"

Bree said, "It won't. Aliens will make sure there is no rain that day."

"You're always talking about aliens," Roman said. "Are you in that Society of Alien Chasers club with Mrs. Lynx?"

"No!" Bree was shocked. "I like aliens."

I glared at Bree. She talked about aliens all the time, and she was going to get my family and me in trouble. Sometimes, my bligfa hurt from worrying about getting caught.

Roman said, "We still need to decide what kind of cake to have."

Just then, the door at the front of the room opened.

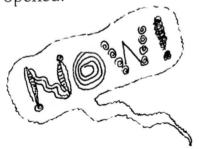

"Now!" Bree whispered to me.

I raced to the classroom's back door, squeezed out, and quietly shut it behind me. In the hallway, I trotted to the boy's bathroom.

I stayed in there a long time.

But finally, I had to come out. I looked toward our classroom. The hallway was empty. I looked toward the office. There was Gloria. She was standing beside Mrs. Lynx, who was looking the U.S. map outside the principal's office. But Gloria was looking straight at me.

She took a step toward me. Her nose lifted, and she sniffed.

I turned and fled back to my class.

At the last second, I looked back. Gloria was tugging at Mrs. Lynx, and she was just starting to turn.

I popped into my classroom. And waited. And waited.

Nothing. I peeked out again. Mrs. Lynx and Gloria were gone.

But now, Mrs. Tarries, the homeroom teacher put a hand on my shoulder. "Kell, where have you been?"

Oh, I groaned. I would have to lie again. I didn't like lying, but when you are an alien on Earth, sometimes you have to.

"I was sick, so I went to the bathroom," I said. "But I am better now."

"OK," Mrs. Tarries said. "Next time tell me when you leave the room. And if you feel bad again, tell me."

"Yes, ma'am," I said.

That night, I helped Roman with his map again. And we worked on it all weekend, too. On Sunday afternoon, we finished.

Roman's map was pretty with all the different colored states. The map's key marked three symbols: black for the borders between each state, blue for water like rivers, lakes and the ocean, and a star for the capital city of each state.

Roman stared and stared at his map. And his smile got bigger and bigger.

I was glad that Roman was ready for Geography Day, which was on Thursday. On Friday, it would be Roman's Giant party at my house, and we still had details to finish.

Roman said, "What about your map? Do you need help?"

"I already did it at home," I told him.

"I've never won anything." Roman ran his hand across his name at the bottom of the map. "But this might be the day."

"You worked hard on it," I said.

"Hey. Thanks for your help," Roman said. "You're a good friend. If you ever need anything, just call me."

Roman was a good Earthling friend. But what if he knew I was an alien? Would he still be my friend? Did I have a real home here on Earth or not?

CHAPTER 6

IDAHO

☆ BOISE

Bang, bang! Ouch!

Dad hit his thumb with a hammer.

It was Sunday night and we were building stilts. For the Giant party, each kid would get a pair of stilts to take home. That meant Dad had to make 30 pairs of stilts before next Friday night.

Dad is very smart and a research scientist and everything. But it is true that he is clumsy. All the wood was cut to the right lengths. He just had to hammer on the small steps that a kid would stand on.

STILTS

Bang, bang! Ouch! Dad hit his thumb.

"Will you paint the stilts?" I asked.

Bang, bang! Ouch! Dad hit his thumb. Again.

"No. We have markers to decorate the stilts. Whoever has the best decorated stilts will get a prize." Dad handed me a piece of wood. "Hold this for me, please."

Bang, bang! Quickly, I moved my hand away so Dad didn't hit my thumb!

Mom opened the back door and called, "John, Dr. East wants to talk to you."

While Dad took the call, I hammered together a stilt all by myself.

Dad came back shaking his head, "Dr. East is worried about the weather. It might rain."

And that's all anyone could talk about. Rain. What if it rained too much for the party? The weather forecast said it was going to rain on Friday night. But Earthling weather forecasters get it wrong all the time. It would probably be sunny and clear on Friday night. We could wait another day or two before we had to think about weather.

Have you ever gotten a song stuck in your head? You sing it over and over? I kept singing, "Twinkle, twinkle, little star, How I wonder what you are." But I couldn't remember the rest of the song.

At lunch on Wednesday, I asked Bree to sing the song again, and I tried to remember more words. But mostly, I just let the Earth sun shine in my heart while she sang. That was a good feeling.

Aja didn't like the singing, though. "Please don't sing while we eat."

Bree told Aja, "That's a good star song."

Aja said, "Why do you care about stars?"

Bree pushed her tray away. She didn't like cafeteria food. "I don't. I just like aliens."

Freddy frowned, "You keep talking about aliens."

Bree glanced at me and turned away, but said nothing. And suddenly, the sun in my heart was covered with clouds.

Aja said, "If you're not eating those fries, can I have them?"

She shoved her tray over to him.

Aja stuffed in fries and mumbled, "Are you an Alien Chaser or an Alien Lover?"

"Yuk," Bree said. "Who would love an alien?"

Now, it was storming in my heart.

All Bree could do was talk about aliens. But it wasn't a joke for me. If anyone else found out I am from Bix, it might be very, very, very, very bad for my family and me. Bree was bad at keeping secrets.

"Enough crazy talk," I said. I picked up my food tray and stomped over to sit with Edgar and Mary Lee.

After school on Wednesday, Mom picked up Bree and me. We only had two days before the Giant party and we had lots of shopping to do. Bree was still singing the "Twinkle, Twinkle" song to herself. Mom asked to hear all of the song. That was OK because I didn't want to talk to Bree.

Jane Taylor
Poet

Bree explained to my mom, "It's really an old poem by Jane Taylor."

Then she sang the whole song.

Twinkle, twinkle, little star,
How I wonder what you are.
Up above the world so high,
Like a diamond in the sky.

When the blazing sun is gone,
When he nothing shines upon,
Then you show your little light,
Twinkle, twinkle, all the night.

Then the traveler in the dark,
Thanks you for your tiny spark,
He could not see which way to go,
If you did not twinkle so.

In the dark blue sky you keep,
And often through my curtains peep,
For you never shut your eye,
'Till the sun is in the sky.

As your bright and tiny spark,
Lights the traveler in the dark.

Though I know not what you are,
Twinkle, twinkle, little star.

Twinkle, twinkle, little star.
  How I wonder what you are.
  Up above the world so high,
  Like a diamond in the sky.

Twinkle, twinkle, little star.
  How I wonder what you are.
  How I wonder what you are.

While she sang, the Earth sun tried to shine in my heart, but I didn't let it. That Bree. She had to stop talking about aliens. Or we couldn't be friends.

Next, we stopped at the candy store.

Mom asked, "Do you have jawbreakers?

"Of course," said Mrs. MeLong. She pulled out three jars that were filled with colorful balls. First there were balls about as big as my thumb. Next were balls about as big as a

quarter. And finally came the giant jawbreakers, bigger than Ping-Pong balls.

Mom bought two of the smallest ones for Bree and me to try. Jawbreakers are candies as hard as a rock.

Mrs. MeLong said, "Don't try to bite it. Just suck."

Bree said, "Aliens have hard teeth. It should be easy for you to bite a jawbreaker."

She was doing it again!

I pulled Bree behind a candy shelf and said, "You don't know how to keep a secret."

Bree said, "I didn't tell anybody—" She looked around, then whispered, "—that you're an alien!"

"But you keep talking about aliens. That means people keep thinking about aliens.

That means they might find out about my family and me. You have to stop."

"But I didn't do anything wrong."

Why didn't she understand? Angry, I said, "We can't be friends. You don't know how to keep a secret."

Bree spit her jawbreaker into her hand. She started to say something else, but I held up my hand and walked away.

Earthling girls just talk too much.

CHAPTER

D ark clouds filled the sky on Geography Day.

Dad came to school with me, so he could bring the extra maps for my friends. He told Mr. Martinez, "I want to donate some prizes."

Prize MAPS

The maps pleased Mr. Martinez. "Who did these? They are excellent."

Dad said, "Oh, we just had these around."

I didn't want anyone to know that I had made the maps. I just wanted my friends to be happy.

Dad added, "I would like to decide who gets these special prizes." That way, we could be sure that my friends got the right maps.

Mr. Martinez nodded. "That's great. You

can be a special judge."

"I'll be back after lunch," Dad said.

On the way to my classroom, it happened. I turned the corner into the Lower Grades Hallway, and there was Gloria and Mrs. Lynx. When she saw me, Gloria's nose went up. She jerked to a stop and pointed her black nose straight at me. Her tail was out straight, and one front paw was pointing at me, too.

Mrs. Lynx kept walking and said, "Come on, Gloria."

But then, she turned back and saw Gloria pointing.

Classes started in ten minutes. Earthlings raced back and forth around me, boys and girls hurrying to their classes.

I put my head down and walked.

Two steps later, Mrs. Lynx called, "Stop! Everyone stop right where you are!"

I kept walking.

"STOP!" Mrs. Lynx bellowed.

My feet froze. I turned and looked at Mrs. Lynx and her dog. This was it.

Behind Gloria was the U.S. map with alien stickers to show where aliens had been found. Would Mrs. Lynx add another sticker today?

Gloria was confused. She still pointed, but her head jerked around, trying to find the alien in the crowd. I was far enough away that I didn't think she could smell me. I looked around, hoping to see another 3rd grader who might have treats for Gloria. But there was no one. I was on my own.

Terrified, I started counting the alien stickers on the U.S. map. 1, 2, 3. . . .

Slowly, I took a baby step backward. 13, 14, 15. . .

Mrs. Lynx bent to stare at each kid, and when she did, I stepped backward again, and again. 18, 19, 20. . . . And then again. 25, 26, 27. . . .

Twenty-seven alien stickers were scattered across the western part of the U.S. How many in the eastern part?

Now, Gloria was pointing straight at me again.

A kindergarten kid started to walk away, but Mrs. Lynx roared, "Stop!"

The kid started wailing, and Mrs. Lynx had to bend down to talk to her.

It was my chance. I turned and darted into my class.

Peeking out, the kindergarten kid was calmer, and now Mrs. Lynx was stooping to look at the next kid.

The final bell rang. Mrs. Lynx stood with her hands on her hips, frowning. Finally, she waved at kids to go to their classes.

That was a close one.

I sat in my seat and shivered. But what about next time? It was hard to be an alien on Earth. It was hard to make friends. It was hard to make a home on a strange planet. It was all hard. At times like this, I just wanted to be home on Bix. Safe.

But I wouldn't know Aja, Freddy, Mary Lee, Roman, or Edgar. Or Bree.

Somehow, I just had to stay hidden.

It was a long morning waiting for the Geography Day assembly. Finally, we lined up to go to the cafeteria.

Mr. Martinez said, "You must be on your best behavior. The food fight on Nutrition Day got many students in trouble."

Some kids laughed. That had been a fun day!

"Try to stay out of trouble this time," Mr. Martinez ordered.

We marched to the cafeteria. The tables were cleaned off, and we laid out our maps for the judges to study.

While the judges worked, we sat on the black and white checkerboard floor. I made sure that I sat far away from Bree. Aja was beside me on one side, and Freddy was on the other side. Onstage, we watched some people do yo-yos. A yo-yo is a wooden or plastic circle that is wrapped with string. An easy thing to do with a yo-yo is make it go up and down. But those yo-yo people did lots more than that.

Freddy asked me, "Why are we watching yo-yos for Geography Day?"

I pointed to the man doing a yo-yo trick. "He said that is called 'Around the World'."

"But what does it have to do with geography?" Freddy said.

Nothing. It was just fun.

When I wasn't watching the yo-yos, I was watching Gloria. She and Mrs. Lynx walked up and down the aisles of maps.

Dad was looking at Roman's map. It was the largest map and had a table by itself. Dad probably liked the stars for each capital city. He was trying to memorize all the U.S. states and capitals.

The judges walked around the room with clipboards. They studied each map and wrote something on their papers.

Suddenly, I heard Mrs. Lynx call out, "Good girl, Gloria."

And there she was, the brown and white pointer dog, the best alien pointer dog in the U.S. She was pointing straight at my Dad.

a thing of beauty... a thing of terror!

Gloria was a thing of beauty. She was a thing of terror.

Quickly, my Dad bent to the dog and started petting her. "Mrs. Lynx, what an interesting dog."

He pulled something out of his pocket. He had doggie treats!

Gloria's tail started wagging, and she dropped her point.

Angrily, Mrs. Lynx said, "This is a working dog. You shouldn't bother her when she is working."

She stared at all the kids sitting on the floor behind my Dad. Roman stood up and said, "Do you need any help?"

Mrs. Lynx looked from Gloria's point to Roman. Her eyes got big, and her mouth looked like she was saying, "Oh!"

Just then, the yo-yo people finished and Mr. Martinez called out, "Time for prizes."

He wrapped his arms around the huge star globe and carried it up the stairs and onto the stage. He set it down on a table, plugged it in and turned on the lights. It was beautiful. And I wished it was mine.

"We've had some special maps donated as consolation prizes," Mr. Martinez announced. "If you didn't win the big prize of the star globe, these prizes should make you happy."

Dad trotted up the stairs to join Mr. Martinez on stage. Dad held up the map on black paper with gold ink.

"This goes to Aja Dalal," Mr. Martinez announced.

Aja went on stage to get the map. Carefully, he touched the gold ink and then fist-pumped.

Mary Lee Glendale got the glow-in-the-dark map next, and Freddy Rubin got the map of the moon's craters. They slapped high-fives.

Which made me grin. I was glad they didn't know the maps came from me.

Bree got her special map of the Rigel star system with Bix marked on it. She looked at me and smiled, but I shook my head. Her smile faded, and she put a finger on her lips. She could keep a secret, she was trying to tell me. But I didn't know if she could stop talking about aliens.

I frowned at her. She frowned at me.

Mr. Martinez tapped the star globe. "Now for the big winner. Roman East."

"No," I whispered. I really wanted that star globe.

As Roman walked by, though, I slapped his hand

and said, "Yes!"

Holding the star globe, the smile on Roman's face was as big and wide as the Earth.

It was a good Geography Day.

After it was over, Dad wound through the crowd to find me. "We have a problem with the Giant party. It's going to rain."

"Maybe it won't."

"The weather man says a 90% chance of rain tomorrow. Yes, it will rain."

"What can we do?"

Dad said, "What on Earth do I know? You have to think of something."

I already had. "Wait here," I said.

I went to the bathroom and pulled a bottle of Dad's cologne from my coat pocket. I poured it on. Oops! The bottle was half gone. I didn't smell like an alien now.

I left the bathroom and went back to the cafeteria to look for Mrs. Lynx.

She was in the middle of the room with Gloria beside her. Would the dog know I was an alien?

I walked straight up to Mrs. Lynx. But my voice didn't work. "Um."

"Yes?" Mrs. Lynx snapped. Her nose twitched.

Gloria wasn't pointing at me. Instead, she was wagging her tail. Had all the treats worked? Or was the cologne working? I didn't care, as long as something worked.

"Did you need something, Kell?" Mrs. Lynx asked. She waved her hand in front of her nose.

Now, the words came fast. "Mrs. Lynx, may Aliens, Inc. use the cafeteria for Roman's Giant party? We will clean it up afterwards. It's just that the weatherman says it will rain, so we can't do it outside. May we use the cafeteria? Please?"

"Are you the one who smells so much?" She bent to look me in the eye.

Those eyes. They were bright blue and shining, eyes that saw everything. I looked down, miserable, and nodded.

Mrs. Lynx stood up straight and pinched her nose shut. Her voice sounded funny, "Yes."

"Yes?" My head jerked up in surprise.

Mrs. Lynx snapped her fingers at Gloria, and the dog lined up beside the principal. "Yes, you may use the cafeteria. Aliens, Inc. does give great parties and it would be a sad thing to cancel one. Have your Dad talk to the school secretary about keys to get in."

Mrs. Lynx looked down at me again with piercing eyes.

I was shocked! The principal's eyes couldn't see everything. They just saw ALMOST everything. I was safe.

"Thank you!" I said.

She nodded and turned away. Walking off, she said, "And Kell—take a bath. You stink."

Roman slapped my back. "The party is saved!"

From across the room, I saw Bree watching. She nodded to me, like she wanted to say, "Good job." But her mouth was straight, and she didn't come and talk to me.

Sometimes Earthling girls talk too much. But sometimes, I just want to hear a certain Earthling girl talking.

CHAPTER 8

The day of the Giant party, it rained.
That morning we decorated the cafeteria and set up the tall striker game. We put non-slip plastic on the bottom of all the stilts, so no one would fall walking on stilts inside. We set up the food tables.

We went home for lunch, and Dad went to pick up some things. Mom went out to check on the bees. She didn't put on her bee clothes or bee hat or bee gloves because honeybees don't like to fly during the rain. They sleep on rainy days. I watched from the window, which was as close as I wanted to get to honeybees.

Mom took the top two hive boxes off to check everything. One or two bees flew around, but the rest were still. She heaved the hive boxes back to the top, but it was wet. They slipped. An angry bee dove and stung her hand.

Back inside, Mom shook water off her hair. She held out her hand and showed me the tiny red spot. "It was my fault," she said.

A few minutes later, though, her hand was bigger. As we watched, it got bigger and bigger. "I must be allergic to bee stings," Mom said.

See? That is why I don't like Earthling bugs.

Mom pulled out her Bixster First Aid kit that we had saved from our space ship. A year ago, the kit was full of small bottles and pills. Now, it was half empty.

Mom looked up, and her silvery eyes were big and scared. "We don't have any *delly* left."

"What's that?"

"It's the medicine for allergies." She coughed, tried to take a deep breath, but coughed again. Now her face looked puffy, too.

That scared me. "Mom," I demanded, "where is Dad?"

"He doesn't answer his phone. He is picking up paper plates and cups for the party." She took another breath, but it sounded rough.

Mom was allergic to the bee sting, and I had to do something. But what?

I bit my lip and worried. "Mom, tell me what to do."

But she was slumped in her chair.

I had to do something. Fast. We needed a doctor, and I only knew one who could help. Quick, I dialed Roman's number.

"Hello."

"Roman, this is Kell. I need to talk to your Dad. My mom is sick."

A moment later, Dr. East said, "Kell. What's wrong?"

"Please, come right now. Mom can't breathe."

"I'll call 911. An ambulance will be there soon."

"NO! You can't do that."

Yes, Kell, if she needs help that fast, you need an ambulance."

I took a deep, shaky breath. "No. The hospital won't know what to do." I didn't want to say it, but I needed help. "We are aliens."

There was silence.

"Please. This isn't a game. We are from space, and Mom will die if you can't help her." Tears filled my eyes.

"I'll be there as fast as I can." The phone went dead.

I ran back to Mom, and she looked really bad. Pale, almost white. Her dark hair looked darker and her face whiter than I had ever seen it.

I picked up Mom's hand, and she squeezed it. Her eyes were closed and she concentrated on each breath. But she squeezed my hand tight.

Suddenly, a flash of light splashed across the windows. Lightning! A deep rumble ran across the sky. Thunder!

Where was Dad?

Where was Dr. East?

Why were we stuck on Earth with all these bugs? I just wanted to be home on Bix where we could go to a doctor and get help.

At last, the doorbell rang and Dr. East ducked to fit through the doorway. He took one look at Mom and jerked open his black bag. He pulled out a needle and a bottle of medicine.

While he pulled medicine into the needle, he said, "You know that this might not work."

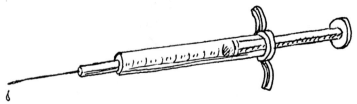

Mom blinked twice and tried to nod that she understood.

But I didn't understand. "What do you mean?"

"This medicine will work on most Earthlings," he said. "But I know nothing about your alien bodies. It might work, or it might make it worse."

Mom gasped, "Do it."

She could barely breathe now. Dr. East was our only hope.

He pushed up her shirt sleeve and rubbed her shoulder with something that smelled funny. Then he jabbed the needle in and gave her the shot.

Mom took a deep breath and leaned back against the chair. Dr. East knelt beside her and watched.

I watched her chest go up and down. Up and—it wasn't moving.

She wasn't breathing.

"Dr. East!"

And then, she drew a shaky breath.

And her breaths came regular. Slowly, she opened her eyes and blinked at me and at Dr. East.

"What will you do?" she whispered.

"I know how to keep secrets," Dr. East said. "But I would like to study your family. It is the chance of a lifetime."

She nodded. "Thank you. But can I talk with John first?"

Dr. East said, "Yes."

And then, my Dad walked in. It took a couple minutes to explain what happened. All he could do was hug my Mom like he would never turn loose.

But Dr. East said, "I think the Giant party starts in an hour."

He was right. And Earthling parties always start on time. We had to hurry.

CHAPTER 9

The Giant party started late. Mom was tired, but she wanted to come and sit and watch the party. We drove through sheets of heavy rain to reach the school.

Dad covered Mom with his jacket to carry her into the cafeteria. I ran after them. Inside, he set Mom down and shook rain from his hair. I shook off rain, took off my jacket and turned around.

The cafeteria was transformed into a Giant Land.

The only lights were floodlights on the floor that pointed upward, which made everything look taller. Dad had set up a kindergarten table for the cake table. Kindergarten chairs were scattered around for seating. The small tables and chairs made the third grade kids seem like giants. And there were true giants walking around. Dr. East's basketball friends were dressed up in giant costumes. There was a hairy Big Foot, a one-eyed Cyclops, and a Paul Bunyan in a red flannel shirt. The

BIG FOOT

giants were all doing yo-yo tricks. When you are that tall, the yo-yo can have a long string!

CYCLOPS

Everyone was already there. Roman saw Dad and waved.

PAUL BUNYON

Dad didn't want to talk to Roman or Mrs. East, though. They were probably mad that we were so late. Instead, Dad got to work. He handed me top-hats to pass out.

I gave one to Bree and she said, "Let me help you."

Grateful, I nodded.

We worked together passing out top hats. Bree is my best friend, and right now, I needed a friend. I whispered and told her about Mom and the bee allergy.

Bree's face was straight and serious. "She will be OK?"

I nodded.

"You did the right thing," Bree said. "I know it was dangerous to tell Dr. East, but you had to get help."

I nodded again. That's the nice thing about Bree. I don't have to talk much.

She said one more thing, "I'm sorry." And she put her finger over her lips.

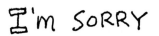

And the Earth's sun shone through all that rain, and my heart was glad that I had an Earthling friend. I smiled.

Bree's face lit up with a huge smile, too.

I said, "Let's do a stilts race. Bet I can beat you."

Bree hit my shoulder and said, "Bet you can't."

I didn't even mind that she hit my shoulder. We just ran toward the other side of the cafeteria where Big Foot was helping kids decorate stilts and learn to walk on them.

But on the way there, I saw Mrs. Lynx talking to my mom. Dad was busy with the cake and punch, so I told Bree, "I need to talk to Mom. I will come to the stilts in a minute."

Mom was sitting in a chair, still tired from the bee allergy.

Mrs. Lynx stood over her and said, "Nice party. Aliens, Inc. does a great job."

Mom nodded, but said, "Where is your dog tonight?"

"My brother will bring her soon," Mrs. Lynx said. Her voice got softer. "We think we will catch aliens tonight. I finally figured it out. The basketball players look like

Earthlings, but Earthlings don't really get that big. It is a good disguise for a giant alien."

"Oh," I said. And I was suddenly glad that Mom, Dad and I were short.

Looking up, I saw the cafeteria door open. Coming in was a white-haired man who was holding Gloria's leash. He looked just like Mrs. Lynx, except shorter and more cheerful. The man and dog both shook off rain. The man looked around and waved.

"There's my brother now. I will introduce you," Mrs. Lynx said.

Mr. Lynx came straight for us.

We should move so Gloria couldn't smell us. But Mom was too weak to jump up and walk around. Mrs. Lynx might think the basketball players were aliens, but Gloria wouldn't be fooled. And I didn't have any doggie treats with me.

The Earthling Society of Alien Chasers was about to win.

CHAPTER 10

No! I couldn't let the S.A.C. win. I pushed through the crowd to the cake table and grabbed Dad. I explained about Mr. Lynx and Gloria.

SAC   MRS. LYNX

SAC   MR. LYNX

SOCIETY
OF
★ALIEN★
CATCHERS

SAC   GLORIA

Quickly, Dad turned around and yelled, "Time for cake!"

The crowd rushed toward the refreshments. Mrs. Lynx tried to push through the crowd to Mr. Lynx, but it was hard to move. Finally, they met in the middle and Mrs. Lynx took Gloria's leash. Mr. Lynx went to sit on the edge of the stage where he was taller than the crowd. He looked all around at the crowd, studying everyone.

I edged along the wall to Mom and helped her walk to another chair by the girl's bathroom. If Gloria came her way, she could duck inside the bathroom.

With Mom safe, we just had to make sure Gloria stayed away from Dad and me.

Dad lit ten candles, and everyone sang, "Happy Birthday to Roman."

Roman leaned down and blew out the candles.

Dad started cutting the cake and passing it out on paper plates.

I handed Roman the first plate. He took a bite and frowned. "Yuk! Carrot cake."

Oh! We never had time to talk about the birthday cake. It was too bad Roman didn't like his own cake. Would he be happy with everything else? Or would he be mad at Aliens, Inc.?

By now, Gloria and Mrs. Lynx were close to the cake table. Soon, she would be able to smell my Dad. But Roman bent to pet Gloria. "She's my friend," he told Mrs. Lynx.

Mrs. Lynx frowned. She probably thought that Gloria should be pointing at Roman, the tall alien kid. But Gloria just wagged her tail. Mrs. Lynx's forehead wrinkled, and she shook her head at her brother. He just shrugged and waved at the basketball player dressed like Paul Bunyan. Mrs. Lynx nodded.

Meanwhile, Roman held his plate down low, and Gloria gulped his cake. She loved it! Her tongue licked the plate. And that gave me an idea. I found my friends and told them to give Gloria their cake, too. And get more and let her eat as much as she wanted.

Mrs. Lynx walked around and let Gloria smell the basketball players dressed like giants. In ten minutes, kids snuck Gloria sixteen pieces of cake. It was better than doggie treats. Her tail dragged. And then, she just sat.

Mrs. Lynx pulled up the leash, but Gloria didn't want to move. She was so full that she just wanted to sleep.

From the other side of the room, Big Foot yelled, "Time for the stilt races."

Everyone sat on the cafeteria floor and left a row down the middle for a racecourse. Dad taped a starting point and an ending point.

Four kids on stilts raced at a time. Next the winners of four races raced. Then those winners raced, until only four stilt walkers were left: Bree, Roman, Aja and Mary Lee.

"On your mark," yelled Big Foot.

The kids stepped up on the stilts.

"Get set. Go!"

ON YOUR MARK,

GET SET.

GO!

Bree and Aja shot out first. Mary Lee was right behind. But Roman had long legs, made even longer by the stilts. Each of his steps was huge. He gained on them.

Gloria staggered onto the racecourse and tried to point. Of course, she was pointing straight at me. But her point fell apart, and she sank to the ground. The kids laughed, and Mr. Lynx quickly moved her off the race course.

Now, Roman was in the lead. And he won!

Roman was smiling and smiling. Aliens, Inc. had done it again. A great party!

And finally, it was time for kids and adults to try the tall striker. Mom sat in a chair beside the tall striker, where she could step on the secret lever.

Kids came and went. Sometimes for small girls like Bree, Mom made it really easy. But mostly, kids had to work to make the bell ring.

When the kids got tired, the adults tried.

Dad picked up the hammer and swung it around a couple times. He heaved it overhead and brought it down on the red circle. Bang! The red arrow went up only halfway. He frowned and tried again. Bang!

I held my breath. Usually the third time, Dad hit his thumb! He swung the hammer and—Bang! The bell still didn't ring. But his thumb was OK.

Mr. Hendricks, Bree's Dad, swung the hammer around and—Smash! No bell.

Bree bounced up and down. "Try again, Dad."

Mr. Hendricks tried again and again while Bree grinned and bounced. Finally, Mr. Hendricks shook his head and handed the hammer to Dr. East.

Dr. East laughed and said, "You two are wimps!" He rubbed his hands together, then picked up the hammer. He swung the hammer, but he was so tall that he swung it at the bell at the top. Bong! The bell rang!

Everyone laughed at his joke.

Mom wanted to try it, too, but Dad said she needed to rest.

Instead, Mrs. Lynx said, "I'll try."

She handed Gloria's leash to her brother,
while she stepped up to the tall striker game.
She wiggled her toes in her toes shoes. The
hammer was heavy for her, but she raised it
high. Bam!

Ding!

Hurrah! The crowd cheered for Mrs. Lynx.
A smile spread across her face, and she
looked almost as cheerful as her brother.

Mr. Lynx hugged her and slapped her
back.

Dad was brave. He asked, "What will you
do with Gloria?"

Mr. Lynx said, "I don't know what is wrong with her. I trained her, but she's not pointing to aliens. I will take her for more training."

Dad nodded, "Good idea."

We were glad that dog was leaving town.

Just then, Mr. and Mrs. Dalal stopped to talk to Mom and Dad.

"This was a very nice party. Aja's birthday is next month. Could you do a surprise party for him?"

Mom said, "A surprise?"

Dad said, "Of course. Aliens, Inc. can do any kind of party you want."

"What kind of surprise party?" Mom asked.

"It doesn't matter," Mrs. Dalal said. "It just matters that he is surprised." She turned to me. "Kell, I know you are friends with Aja. You must not tell him anything."

"I promise," I said. "It will be a big surprise to him."

Mrs. Lynx had been listening to Mr. and Mrs. Dalal. She said, "Mrs. Smith, I have some party ideas. I'll call you later with some suggestions."

"Thank you," Mom said.

Now, almost everyone had gone home. Bree was helping me mop the cafeteria floor. Roman's Dad was talking to Mom, checking to see how she felt.

Roman asked me, "Did Mrs. Lynx catch any aliens today?"

"No," I said. "She thought your family was alien because you are all so tall."

"That's funny. Because the only aliens around here are short."

I looked up and leaned on the mop handle. "Your Dad told you?"

"No. When you helped me jump out of Texas, I guessed it. That's why I kept playing with Gloria so much, to keep her away from you."

"Thanks."

"I just have one request," Roman said.

"What?"

"Could you wear your Dad's cologne every day? It would smell better."

Bree laughed. "It is true. Alien boys stink almost as much as Earthling boys."

The End

FOR FUN

THERE ARE 11 STATE MAPS HIDDEN SOMEWHERE WITHIN THE PAGES OF THIS BOOK. CAN YOU FIND ALL OF THEM? DO YOU KNOW THE CAPITAL OF EACH STATE?

The Answers are at MimsHouse.com/aliens

Join Our Mailing List.

MimsHouse.com/newsletter/

Other Books in The Aliens, Inc. Series

Book 1: *Kell, the Alien*
Book 2: *Kell and the Horse Apple Parade*
Book 3: *Kell and the Giants*
Book 4: *Kell and the Detectives (2015)*

Other Books by Darcy Pattison

Saucy and Bubba: A Hansel and Gretel Tale

The Girl, the Gypsy and the Gargyole

Vagabonds

Abayomi, the Brazilian Puma:

Wisdom, the Midway Albatross:

The Scary Slopes

Prairie Storms

Desert Baths

19 Girls and Me

Searching for Oliver K. Woodman

The Journey of Oliver K. Woodman

The River Dragon

MEET KELL SMITH, ALIEN

MEET KELL'S FRIENDS

Aliens, Inc. Series: Book 1
Kell, the Alien

Shipwrecked on earth and desperate to make money, an alien family decides to make a living by opening Aliens, Inc., an intergalactic event-planning business master-minded by 9 year old alien boy, Kell Smith.

Darcy Pattison
Rich Davis

Kell discovers that his neighbor, Bree Hendricks, turns 9-years-old next month and she wants a party with an alien theme. That should be simple as flying from star to star. But things aren't that easy: Earthling's ideas about aliens are totally wrong. Even worse,

Principal Lynx is a UFO-Chaser and suspects aliens around every corner.

Will the Aliens totally blow the Aliens Party? Will Principal Lynx capture Kell and his family and them over to the government?

Aliens, Inc. Series: Book 2
Kell and the Horse Apple Parade

Kell, Bree, and the Alien, Inc. gang return to plan a new event, a Friends of Police parade. But Principal Lynx believes someone in third grade is an alien, and she scans each student with her new Alien Catcher App. Kell and Bree deal with  City Hall, figure out fund-raising, and keep the Parade marching. When the Society of Alien Chasers (S.A.C.) attends the Parade, Kell must find a way to keep his family safe. Join the fun-loving aliens from planet Bix for another out-of-this world adventure.

ABOUT THE AUTHOR & ILLUSTRATOR

Translated into eight languages, children's book author DARCY PATTISON writes picture books, middle grade novels, and children's nonfiction. Previous titles include *The Journey of Oliver K. Woodman* (Harcourt), *Searching for Oliver K. Woodman* (Harcourt), *The Wayfinder* (Greenwillow), *19 Girls and Me* (Philomel), *Prairie Storms* (Sylvan Dell), *Desert Baths* (Desert Baths), and *Wisdom, the Midway Albatross* (Mims House.) Her work has been recognized by **starred reviews** in *Kirkus*, *BCCB*, and *PW*. *Desert Baths* was named a 2013 Outstanding Science Trade Book and the *Library Media Connection*, Editor's Choice. She is a member of the Society of Children's Bookwriters and Illustrators and the Author's Guild. For more information, see darcypattison.com.

RICH DAVIS, illustrator for the Aliens, Inc series has wondered, "What could be better than getting to do black and white cartoon work for a sci-fi easy reader?" Working on this book has been one big fun-making experience. Rich has also illustrated 12 other children's books, including beginning reader series, *Tiny the Big Dog* (Penguin). His joy is to help kids develop creatively and he has invented a simple drawing game (Pick and Draw.com) and an activities book as a fun tool that now have a following around the world. He frequently does programs at schools and libraries in order to draw with thousands of kids yearly. For him, it is a dream come true and he recognizes that the source is from God alone.

CPSIA information can be obtained at www.ICGtesting.com
Printed in the USA
LVOW10s1451210714

395323LV00001B/166/P